A pukelear explosion . . .

"They don't call him Bigfart for nothing!" Mr. Brill went on. "He farts only once per year. He chooses one victim, one unlucky camper, and hits him full blast with the buttal explosion to end all buttal explosions. We're talking a force-ten farticane."

Eight . . . seven . . .

My head was swimming. I was halfway through the countdown to a pukelear explosion in the megachunk range. But at the same time I was too terrified to move. My legs had turned to overcooked spaghetti.

And still Mr. Brill went on. His voice was weird. There was an insane edge to it.

Six . . . five . . .

Don't miss any of the books in

—the totally
GROSS
and hilariously funny
new series from Bantam Books!

1 The Great Puke-off

2 The Legend of Bigfart

3 Mucus Mansion

Coming soon:

4 Garbage Time

5 Dog Doo Afternoon

6 To Wee Or Not To Wee

THE LEGEND OF BIGFART

BY
PAT POLLARI

BANTAM BOOKS
NEW YORK • TORONTO • LONDON • SYDNEY • AUCKLAND

BARF-O-RAMA: THE LEGEND OF BIGFART
A BANTAM BOOK : 0 553 50558 0

First published in USA by Bantam Books, 1996
First publication in Great Britain

PRINTING HISTORY
Bantam edition published 1997

Barf-O-Rama™ is a trademark of
Daniel Weiss Associates, Inc. and is used under license

Produced by Daniel Weiss Associates, Inc.
33 West 17th Street, New York, NY 10011, USA.

Bantam Books are published by Transworld Publishers Ltd,
61–63 Uxbridge Road, Ealing, London W5 5SA,
in Australia by Transworld Publishers (Australia) Pty Ltd,
15–25 Helles Avenue, Moorebank, NSW 2170,
and in New Zealand by Transworld Publishers (NZ) Ltd,
3 William Pickering Drive, Albany, Auckland.

Printed and bound in Great Britain by
Cox & Wyman Ltd, Reading, Berkshire.

To Michael

ONE

Okay, I admit it: I was a wuss. Absolute truth. I was the most pathetic human being on earth.

I had two huge problems. First, I was a total coward.

How big a coward? Let me put it this way—the list of things I was afraid of included not just your basic ghosts and goblins and slashers and spiders and bugs. Most people are afraid of those kinds of things. Me? I was afraid of stuffed animals.

Stuffed animals weren't the only things that scared me; I'm just using that as an example of how bad off I was. I mean, come on. Stuffed animals? But they made me shiver. It was the eyes, mostly.

My other problem was that I had this delicate stomach. Almost anything made me sick. Cheese made me sick. Raisins made me sick. Even the thought of coleslaw made me sick.

And yogurt? Being in the same room with yogurt practically made me heave.

I don't mean to sound like a show-off or anything, but I could have been in *The Guinness Book of Records* as the greatest barfer, heaver, chunk blower, upchucker, extruder, stomach-content emitter, and all-around vomiter in history. I mean, I did the blew magoo at least three or four times a day. More when my little sister would watch Barney on TV.

So basically for me, life just swung back and forth between terror and nausea. Shivering and barfing. Shaking and chucking. It was no kind of life for a kid who was going to be moving into junior high. From everything I had heard, junior high pretty much made everyone sick—even tough kids.

I figured junior high would destroy me. Only something else got to me first, before junior high.

Summer camp.

My name is Robert. Some people called me Bob. Some people called me Bobby.

And some called me *Baby*.

My last name is Warmack, which leads to "Worm."

Yes, people called me Baby Worm.

Not everyone called me that. My parents didn't. Teachers didn't. At least not where I could hear them. I figure approximately half the kids in my fifth-grade class called me by my right name.

That would be the fifty percent that are girls. Girls are usually nice to me.

It would be the guy half of the class that called me Baby Worm.

My story begins on the last day of school. A long, long time ago. At least a couple of months.

I was walking along between classes, minding my own business, with my hands in my pockets so I wouldn't pick up any germs. (Yes, I was afraid of germs, too.) Suddenly, out of nowhere, there were these three guys—Hedley Hampton, Jamal Ishiyama, and Buttfire Tisch. They grabbed me and shoved me into the boys' room.

"Got him," Jamal said. Then he started doing this strange laugh he has. It's like, "Ga-hunh, ga-hunh, ga-hunh."

Jamal's not going to be a nuclear physicist, if you know what I mean. Although he's practically a genius compared to Buttfire Tisch.

"Baby *Worm*," Buttfire said. "Baby *W-o-o-o-r-m*."

Buttfire got his nickname by lighting one of his farts. I guess it didn't work the way it was supposed to because Buttfire (whose real name is Marion) ended up in the hospital for two weeks.

Hedley Hampton was the brains of the threesome. He was plenty smart in an evil, devious, rotten sort of way.

Hedley put his arm around my shoulders. "Boys, boys! Now, don't be referring to our friend Robert by that demeaning appellation. 'Baby Worm'! What a terrible thing to say to our homie Robert."

I wasn't stupid enough to believe that Hedley was being sincere. I may have been a coward, but I wasn't an idiot.

"Listen up, Baby . . . I mean, Robert," Hedley said. "We have a little problem. We were wondering if you might have the time to help us out. I *so* admire your intelligence. I'd be honored if you'd give me the benefit of your insight."

"Hedley, take a hike, you loser," I said. "Don't make me hurt you."

Okay, that's not exactly what I said.

What I actually said was, "Um o-o-o um o-uh-o-o-kay, H-Hed-Hedley."

Hedley leaned close. He put his face right up in front of mine. He has a kind of chubby face with bright cheeks and sparkly blue eyes. You'd never guess to look at him what a creep he is.

"See, my friend Buttfire here, he accidentally dropped his favorite pen in the toilet. *This* toilet." He suddenly yanked me over to one of the stalls and kicked open the door.

"Ga-hunh, ga-hunh," Jamal commented.

At least Jamal thought it was funny. I didn't. I was shaking in my shoes.

"The problem we have is this," Hedley went on. "As you can see, the pen is still in the toilet. Unfortunately Buttfire left a little something *else* in there, too. Perhaps you've noticed a certain . . . aroma?"

I had noticed the aroma. It was impossible not to. And I knew what I would see when I looked down into that porcelain swimming pool.

It lay there in the toilet bowl like a coiled snake: the brown substance.

I gulped hard. "Y-y-y-es, I-I-I, um, I no-ticed." I was fighting hard not to heave. But the sight of that putrid butt sausage . . . I mean, if cheese could make me gack, you *know* that poop snake, coiled around that worthless pen, wasn't going to calm my jumpy stomach down.

And we're talking the most foul poopto-nium you could possibly imagine. Radioactive. Deadly at a distance of ten feet. It would still be deadly in the year two thousand and fifty.

"Well, here is our dilemma," Hedley said, his voice slithering like a lizard's tongue. "We don't want to flush, or the pen will be lost. And yet no one wants to put his hand in there to get it out."

I was quivering with fear. My heart was beating like a bunny who's just realized he's surrounded by hungry wolves. It was a race to see which would get me first—the fear or the need to heave. My stomach had rented a U-Haul and relocated to my throat.

"*You* want to stick your hand in there and get that pen, Jamal?" Hedley asked Jamal.

"Ga-hunh. No way. Ga-hunh. Ga-hunh."

"How about you, Buttfire?"

"Huh?" Buttfire asked. "Um, no."

"See? No one wants to toilet dive for that pen," Hedley said. "I was depressed when I realized this. Then I thought, Hey! What we need is someone with the courage to perform this toilet dive. And who would be a better toilet diver than our good friend Robert Warmack? Robert, who we all know is brave and has such a strong stomach."

"Noooooo," I began to moan.

I tried to squirm out of Hedley's pudgy grip. But Jamal and Buttfire grabbed me. They lifted me off my feet. I kicked at the air.

Then they turned me over. Upside down. Quarters fell out of my pockets and plopped onto the buttwurst. One showed heads. One showed tails.

"Okay," Hedley said to me. "Go fish!"

I saw the toilet bowl directly below me.

I saw what was *in* the toilet bowl.

The stench rose up like a fist.

I began to cry. "Nooooo! Nooooo!"

But surprisingly enough, Hedley, Jamal, and Buttfire were not moved by my pleas.

My head descended toward the toilet. I tried to grab onto the toilet seat.

I was helpless. I was terrified. I was sick.

"Nooooo!"

"Yeeees!" Hedley said gleefully. "In you go, Baby Worm! In you go!"

It began. The shaking that always hits when I'm most afraid. And at the same time my stomach began the warm-up for the blew magoo.

"He's gonna blow!" Hedley cried out triumphantly.

My guts began to do the wiggle. My throat began the gack dance. It was five seconds to launch. Four . . . three . . .

"*Huhhghg huhhgh huhhgh*—" I began.

"He can't stop it now!" Hedley yelled joyously.

He was right. Two . . . one . . .

I blew chunks. I magooed. I showed everyone my breakfast. "*Huhhghg b-b-bub-bleeeeeaaaaah!*"

The barf poured from my mouth like Niagara Falls.

It shot out, then dribbled down my face. Into my hair. Into my nose. I was temporarily blinded by half-digested oatmeal.

"Now let him go!" Hedley cried gleefully.

Hands released my ankles. Gravity took over.

Down I fell into the toilet. Into a soup of steaming barf and reeking brown substance. The sound of my own cries echoed in the toilet bowl.

It was not one of the high points of my life.

But what Hedley didn't know, and even I didn't know at that point, was that Baby Worm . . . was about to turn.

TWO

"No! You can't really mean it! Nooooooo!" I wailed. "Not summer camp!"

It was two hours later. I had almost gotten the reek off me. Almost. And I was looking forward to some peace in the safety of my room. But nooooo, that would be too easy.

"Dad, don't! Don't make me!" I cried.

But my father was no more impressed by my pathetic cries than Hedley and his pals had been.

See, my dad is a Marine. And not just any old Marine—he's in some special parachute squad that jumps from airplanes and lands behind enemy lines. Except that they usually refuse to use the parachutes because that makes it too easy.

"Look, Robert," he said, "it's time for you to grow up. You are going to camp, and that's all there is to it."

"But Dad, I can't go to summer camp! I won't know any of the kids there. I won't like the food. I won't be able to fall asleep in a strange bed. Remember the time I had to sleep at Grandma's and I was up all night? Do you want me to die from lack of REM?"

"Maybe we should reconsider, dear," my mother said.

Good old Mom. She's always on my side.

"We are *not* reconsidering," my dad said firmly. "We agreed. It's time to cut the apron strings. A boy needs to learn some independence if he's ever going to become a man."

"I don't want to be independent!" I whimpered. "I don't want to be a man!"

Yeah, I know. Pretty sickening, right? But at the time I was just terrified of the idea of camp. It was like regular life was bad enough, you know? And now my parents wanted to make it even worse.

"You leave next week, Robert. Next Saturday at oh nine hundred hours, to be

12

precise. That's nine A.M. You're going to Camp Winnapuke."

For the next week I tried every trick I knew to convince my parents to change their minds. I whined. I wept. I wheedled. I pretended I had cancer, the measles, anything and everything. But then, the more I thought about *pretending* to be sick, the more I worried I would *really* get sick, which just made me nauseous.

So I gave up pretending. I went back to pleading for mercy. As I saw that dreaded Saturday deadline approaching I pulled out all the stops. I abandoned my last tiny shred of self-respect and just wallowed and groveled like a worm. But nothing worked.

The week passed. My parents bought me a notebook and some stamps so I could write them letters. I knew I was doomed.

Then it was Saturday.

My parents woke me up at seven thirty. I tried to pretend I was paralyzed. But that didn't work either. My dad just waved a piece of American cheese at me and I ran for the toilet.

My mom was crying when I left the house. At least I think she was. It was hard to tell over the sound of my own loud wailing.

My dad drove me to the place where the buses came to collect kids for camp. But just before we got there, he did something strange. He pulled over to the side of the road and turned off the engine.

"Son," he said.

"Yes?" I said hopefully. I thought, Okay, maybe he's changed his mind.

"Son, you know what I do for a living, right?"

"Sure."

"And you know I've got a lot of medals and stuff. Things that prove how brave and how tough I am. Medals for heroism. Medals for getting hurt. Medals for that time I was behind enemy lines and had to live on nothing but beetles and pig sweat."

I could feel my stomach starting to squirm. I hated that story about the beetles and pig sweat. "Yeah, Dad," I said glumly. "I know you're brave and tough and nothing makes you sick. But I'm just not like you. I'm not brave and tough. I'm a coward. I can't eat beetles. Just thinking about it . . ."

"Roll down the window!" he yelled.

I rolled it down and stuck my head out. "*Bleah. Uuuu-g-g-g-BLEAH!*" I spewed out into the fresh morning air. It wasn't a huge spew. Just kind of a moderate extrusion.

"Are you done?" my dad asked.

I nodded. "Just don't tell any more war stories, okay?"

"I was trying to make a point, Robert. See, I know you think I'm this big, strong guy who can handle anything. But what you don't realize is that I used to be just like you."

I wiped a stray chunk of stomach contents from my lips. "You mean you were a weak-stomached coward?" I said bitterly.

"Exactly. A pathetic pusillanimous puker."

Good old Dad. He doesn't really believe in all that stuff about being supportive and positive to your kids.

"Where do you think you got those qualities?" my father asked. "You got them from *my* side of the family. You inherited them from me."

I was stunned. I couldn't believe that my dad would share this story with me. That he would trust me with his own tale of geekhood. I suddenly felt really close to him.

15

So I said, "Does that mean I don't have to go to camp? Please, please, please, oh please?"

He rolled his eyes. "No, Robert. You're not listening. I'm telling you: I used to be just like you. Until one summer my dad made me go to summer camp. In fact, it was Camp Winnapuke. The same camp you're going to."

I looked at him suspiciously.

"See, son, it was my time at Camp Winnapuke that made me the man I am today. Before that I was a sniveling, gutless worm with a stomach so weak I used to woof up a kidney at the very mention of oysters."

I thought of what he was trying to say. Then I thought of oysters. All gray and slimy, like a glob of snot on the half shell . . .

"Roll down the window!" my dad ordered.

When I was done, he looked me straight in the eye. "Trust me on this. Camp Winnapuke will change the way you live your life." He smiled at me mysteriously. "You may find that by facing the thing you fear most—the most nauseating, sickening, disgusting thing in the world—you'll get to a place beyond fear, beyond even the urge to purge."

"So you're saying I still have to go?"

I was blubbering pretty good by the time the bus came. It was okay, though, because there were other kids crying, too. Of course they were all a couple of years younger than me.

But I was trying to stop my weeping because I was hoping that maybe . . . just maybe . . . my dad was right. Maybe camp would change everything. Maybe I would become a new kind of person. Maybe I would get all the other kids to like and respect me. Maybe . . .

Or not.

I climbed on the bus. And then through my tears I saw something that made me twice as scared, and three times as sick, as I'd been up till then.

The something was sitting in the back of the bus: Hedley Hampton. And Jamal Ishiyama. And Buttfire Tisch.

Instantly the memory of my terrible toilet dive came flooding back to me. Once again I saw that terrifying buttwurst. Once again the death reek of ripe brown substance came back. I reeled. I fell into the nearest seat.

I could feel my stomach begin to squish like a water balloon. The countdown to launch started. Ten . . . nine . . . eight . . .

We have gack dance!

Seven . . . six . . .

Stomach pressure at maximum!

I looked at the person in the seat beside me. It was a girl with red hair. She was kind of pretty.

"Window . . ." I said in a low voice. "The window . . ."

She looked closely at me. "You look like you're ready to spew," she said.

I nodded. In my head the countdown was moving onward, unstoppable!

Five . . . four . . . three . . .

Suddenly the girl grabbed the window. "Hold on!" she yelled. She tried to yank the window down, but it was stuck!

Two . . . one . . .

I gritted my teeth.

"No," the girl cried. "Don't vomitize me!"

Down came the window with a bang, but too late!

Blastoff!

I blew like a volcano. I was Mount Vomituvious. I was Pukatao.

My teeth were still gritted tightly. But it was no use. There's no stopping the force of nature.

Barf squirted through the cracks between my teeth. The force of it blew out a front tooth that was kind of loose anyway. The tooth flew through the air and landed in the girl's red hair.

Right behind it came hot stomach contents. It shot through the hole in my teeth like a fire hose. The spray hit the girl in the face. Desperately I turned away, but the puke stream sprayed across the kids sitting in front of me.

"Oh, yagh! Yagh! Gross! YUCK!" they screamed.

In total panic I turned the other way and hosed the kids across the aisle.

"No! Get away from me! No! NOOO!"

The pressure let up. I swallowed all the vomit I could, but mostly it was spread all around me.

I surveyed the damage I had done. Sixteen kids had been hit by the guttal explosion.

Their hair dripped with my chunks. My steaming gumbo slithered down their faces.

Then I realized there was someone standing over me: Hedley. Followed by Buttfire and Jamal. None of them had been hit.

"Well, well, well," Hedley said in a loud voice. "Up to your usual tricks, eh? Everyone? Everyone, may I have your attention?"

He didn't need to get everyone's attention, trust me. They had already noticed me. Especially the kids I'd heaved all over.

"This is Baby Worm," Hedley said gleefully.

The dreaded nickname reverberated around the bus. I could hear kids repeating it. "Baby Worm . . . Baby Worm."

The bus driver didn't seem to notice the hysteria and violent chucking. He was too busy flipping a floppy goober out of his nose. He revved the engine and the bus started moving.

I was on my way to camp. On my way to camp, accompanied by three guys who loved to torture me. And I had already blown breakfast all over everyone within range, which was not going to help me to become popular.

So far the whole experience was turning out even worse than I had expected. And I wasn't even out of the parking lot yet.

THREE

"Sweet Jasper! Ugh! What happened in here?"

The bus had arrived at the camp after a twisting, turning ride up mountain roads. Finally we stopped. The door opened. A man climbed on. A very hairy man. I mean, I'm serious. This guy was hairy. And in all the wrong places.

He looked around the bus. I guess it did look a little strange. I mean, there I was, sitting all alone, amid the devastation caused by my guttal explosion. Everyone else was crowded as far from me as they could get. Except the red-haired girl. She had only moved across the aisle.

And there was the smell. You can probably

imagine what puke, trapped in a hot bus for several hours, smells like.

It wasn't exactly April fresh in there.

"My name is Mr. Brill," the hairy guy said. "I run Camp Winnapuke. I'm the boss. While you're here at camp, you will obey me, and you will obey all the counselors. When I say 'jump,' all you ask is 'how high?' Do I make myself clear?"

"As clear as an unmuddied lake," Hedley Hampton said.

Mr. Brill gave him a dirty look. "You back talking me, son?"

"My name is Hedley Hampton," Hedley said. Then he repeated it, slowly. "Hedley *Hampton*."

The change in Mr. Brill's attitude was total. "Hampton?" he said. A greasy smile broke out on his hard face. "Yes, I know your father well. All the arrangements have been made."

I got a real bad feeling right about then. I mean, okay, it wasn't like I had done much to make myself popular and well liked so far. But now it looked like Hedley had some kind of special relationship with the camp owner. That wasn't going to help at all.

Or maybe I was jumping to conclusions.

Mr. Brill said, "Hedley, why don't you and your friends get off this stinking bus and out into the fresh air? This must have been a terrible ordeal for you."

Hedley, Buttfire, and Jamal stood up and walked down the aisle. The girl with the red hair (who still had my tooth stuck in her bangs) started to get up, too.

"No!" Mr. Brill yelled. "The rest of you sit down. I'll tell you when you can move. Until then, SIT!"

The girl sat down fast.

Okay, so maybe I wasn't jumping to conclusions.

Hedley paraded past me like Mr. America and stepped off the bus. Mr. Brill hurried after him.

The red-haired girl looked at me questioningly. I shrugged. "Hedley's rich. His dad owns the company that makes the paper rolls in toilet paper and paper towels. They're really powerful."

"It's not fair," the girl said. She looked angry. "My name's Penny, by the way."

"Robert Warmack," I said, introducing myself. "Sorry I blew stomach contents all over you."

"I guess that kind of thing happens to everyone once in a while," she said.

I was about to say, "Once in a while? Try several times a day." But she was at least talking to me. And she seemed nice. So I didn't see any reason to frighten her.

What I said was, "Thanks." And then I reached toward her.

She cringed back. I guess that was understandable.

"I just wanted to get this out of your hair," I said. I reached again and removed the tooth from her bangs. I held it up so she could see what I'd done.

She looked somewhat disgusted. But she forced a smile anyway. That smile made me feel good. I knew it was a "pity" smile, but I'd take what I could get.

With Hedley safely escorted from the bus, Mr. Brill got back on. He was followed by a big high school kid who had a face like oatmeal mixed with strawberries. Serious acne.

"This is my right-hand man," Mr. Brill announced.

"That's right," the high-school guy said. "My name is Dreezer. For the next two weeks I am your MASTER! Do you understand?"

Most of the kids just kind of shrugged. I nodded real fast because he scared me.

"Good. 'Cause when you mess with the Dreeze, you get the squeeze. Got me?"

Actually I had no idea what that was supposed to mean. Besides, I was kind of fixated on his zits. And they were making me sick again. Fortunately I was on empty—nothing left to blow.

They marched us off the bus and I got my first good look around. The camp was half a dozen log cabins spread around under the trees. There was a main building, also made out of logs but a lot bigger. And there was a lake, with a little dock and some canoes.

I guess it was an okay place. If you weren't afraid of the woods. And if you weren't terrified of water because you worried about drowning. And if you weren't shaky just from thinking about all the wild animals: skunks and possums and deer.

Don't laugh—deer have ticks. Bloodsucking, diseased ticks. I bet you didn't think about that. You were probably thinking about Bambi. Well, guess what—Bambi may not have ticks, but real deer do.

But what really worried me was the small

building standing alone by the edge of the woods. It was too small to be a cabin. It had two doors. On one door there was a sign that said Girls and on the other a sign that said oys. I guess the *B* fell off.

"An outhouse!" I whispered in horror. I knew such things existed, but I never expected to have to use one.

They called out our names, and we were sent to the different cabins carrying our few possessions. Boys went to certain cabins and girls to others. This was depressing, because Penny was a girl. And she was the closest thing I had to a friend at Camp Winnapuke.

The cabins looked worse inside than out. There were cots lined up on both sides. We each had a little footlocker we could put our stuff in.

It was a dismal-looking place, I have to say. Just cots and lockers and a bunch of lost-looking kids. Some people were even crying.

Okay, *I* was crying. But some of the other kids probably would have been crying, too, only they had too much pride.

At the far end of the cabin there were three regular beds. They were near the only windows. They were made up with expensive quilts. There was a TV there as well.

My first thought was: Okay, this must be for the counselors.

But no, that was wrong. Those beds and the TV set were for Hedley and his henchmen.

I couldn't believe it! I was cursed. Not only did I have to go to camp. Not only was Hedley going to the same camp. Hedley was in my cabin!

Hedley saw me staring at him.

"Hey, Robert. You got a problem or something?"

"Me? No. No, of course I don't have a problem. I . . . I was just . . ."

"You were just *what*?"

"It's just, maybe I should try to get into one of the other cabins."

"No way, Robert." Hedley snickered. "No way."

"But why? I mean, you can't stand me. You despise me. All you ever do is torture me. Why don't you want me to leave?"

Hedley grinned his evil grin. "Maybe I *like* torturing you, Baby Worm."

The way he looked at me, I got scared all over again.

Then Dreezer came in, followed by two other camp counselors, a guy and a girl.

"Listen up," Dreezer said. "I imagine you're all pretty hungry after your long bus ride. Especially certain people who squirted their breakfasts all over the bus." He looked at me and laughed. "So it's noon. And at noon we eat lunch. Everyone over to the main building. NOW!"

We all took off. I was glad to see that even some of the other kids were a little scared of Dreezer.

Outside I saw Penny again. She was in line to go into the main building. I went and stood with her.

"How's your cabin?" I asked.

"Fine, I guess," she said. "If you like bare floors and bare walls and scratchy sheets and no TV."

"It's the same in my cabin."

"I hope they at least give us something decent to eat," she said.

I just nodded. "I hope it isn't something that will make me sick."

Penny looked at me a little suspiciously. "What do you mean?"

I shrugged. "I guess I have kind of a delicate

stomach. Lots of stuff makes me sick."

"Like what?"

"Well, the problem is, if I tell you all the stuff that makes me sick, it'll make me sick. You know, just from thinking about it."

"Okay. How about this: what *doesn't* make you sick?"

"Oh, that's a smaller list. Like . . . um, ice cream. But not frozen . . . you know, the frozen stuff that's like ice cream?"

"Frozen yogurt?"

She had said the *Y* word: *yogurt*. I felt the first steps of the gack dance. But like I said, I was on empty.

She shook her head. "You're kind of a mess, aren't you?"

I nodded. "I guess so."

"Look, here's what you do: whatever you eat, just close your eyes, hold your nose so you can't smell it, and keep telling yourself, It's ice cream. It's just ice cream."

"You mean, pretend it's ice cream?"

"You said you like ice cream, so pretend it's ice cream."

I was amazed. It seemed so simple. Could it possibly work? If it did, why, my life would be transformed. I had hope. Actual hope!

I looked at her and smiled. "I'll try it!"

"Great," Penny said. "And just to show you how confident I am, I'm going to sit right across from you."

"Ice cream," I said. "The whole world is ice cream. It's so simple!"

FOUR

"Everything is ice cream," I repeated as we were marched inside. "Everything is ice cream." I was going to triumph over my weak stomach by a simple act of will.

If this worked, Penny and I could go on TV and do an infomercial for the idea. We could call it ice cream therapy.

The main building was much larger than the cabins we slept in. There were about a dozen long tables with benches. Sort of like picnic tables, only we were inside, not outside.

There was a long, stainless steel counter where we picked up the food. It was just like the cafeteria at school, only instead of lunch ladies wearing hair nets, we had high-school- and college-age guys and girls wearing stained T-shirts with the name of the camp on them.

But the food . . . the food was the same.

Bucket after bucket of gooey substances that stuck to the spoon like snot when the server ladled them up.

Tray after tray of deep-fried mystery globules, dripping grease.

Reeking piles of gray-green vegetables, sending their nauseating reek wafting toward my nose.

Then I recognized one particular smell. It was the stench of the most horrifying food substance in my entire long list of horrifying food substances.

Brussels sprouts!

I tried not to look, but you know how it's hard to look away from a gruesome accident even though you know you shouldn't look? Well, that's how it was.

I knew I shouldn't look, but I did. And there they were: round little bundles of tightly packed gray-green leaves.

"Brussels sprouts," I moaned.

"Let me guess: you don't like brussels sprouts," Penny said.

I shook my head violently. "It all . . . it all began with brussels sprouts. It . . . it's my most painful memory."

As we advanced down the line I told my sad tale.

It happened back when I was just six. Six was a very important age for me. You see, that's when my problem became obvious. That's when I learned that I was destined to become the barf king.

My mom and dad had invited some people over for dinner. The pastor from our church and his wife. They were nice enough people, I guess. Pastor Roberson and Mrs. Roberson were old enough to have wrinkles. Also, there was something funny about the pastor's hair. It seemed kind of stiff, like maybe it was made out of the same fabric as the carpet in our family room.

Well, anyway, we were all sitting at the table. Pastor Roberson kept asking me if I was enjoying first grade. Like anyone ever in all of history ever actually enjoyed first grade. But I was trying to be polite, so I said yes. Yes, I loved first grade.

Then my mom started carrying in these big platters of food.

A big platter of ham, all pink and quivering. Back then ham didn't bother me. Of course that was *before* I saw that movie *Babe*.

So anyway, my mom came in with the ham and a plate of baked potatoes. Baked potatoes are okay as long as you don't put anything on them. And finally she brought in the brussels sprouts.

Brussels sprouts always announce the fact that they're coming. The stench of brussels sprouts gets there about a minute ahead of the actual sprouts. The stench is kind of like the announcer or the veejay. "Hey, we got a little something coming up next that you're *really* going to hate."

But see, this was when I was young. So I didn't just instantly huff up an intestine, like I would now. Plus, this was my very first exposure to an actual brussels sprout.

I didn't know about brussels sprouts. That's the tragedy: I DIDN'T *KNOW!*

Mom loaded up my plate.

The pastor was chatting away.

Mrs. Roberson was making small talk about

something or other. Charity or good works or whatever.

And then, it all happened at once.

My mom said, "Robert, eat your brussels sprouts."

Like a good little boy, I popped one in my mouth.

Mrs. Roberson said something like, "So, what we hope to do is buy new silk vestments for the—"

Then the taste of brussels sprout hit my taste buds.

Mrs. Roberson opened her mouth to say *altar,* and as she did, her upper teeth started to wiggle away from her gums.

Dentures! Loose dentures!

The hellish flavor of brussels sprouts!

Slimy fake teeth!

Brussels sprouts!

I gagged. I tried to hold it down, but I was powerless before the power of puke. The brussels sprout shot out of my mouth like the cork in a champagne bottle.

"BLEAH!"

The sprout went flying through the air. It was a green cannonball!

The sprout hit Mrs. Roberson right in the

mouth. Her false teeth clamped down on the evil green nodule.

And then Mrs. Roberson's teeth, firmly clamped onto the brussels sprout, fell out *into* the platter of sprouts!

Fake pink gums, dripping with spit, were arrayed on a backdrop of brussels sprouts!

But the horror wasn't over yet.

I did the blew magoo. Maximum gaggage.

It was too late to find a place to unload. So I grabbed the first thing I could find: the bowl of brussels sprouts. And I went from half full to empty in about two seconds.

And that's when Pastor Roberson decided he'd had enough. He jumped up, scrambling to get back out of the way.

His head hit the chandelier.

The chandelier scraped the wig from his head. It fell like a dying squirrel shot from a tree.

It fell into the sprouts.

That image . . . I've never been able to forget that image. Glistening pink dentures and ratty hair, nestled on a bed of brussels sprouts, with a vomit sauce.

It all started that night. It all started with brussels sprouts.

*　　*　　*

And now, years later at a camp far from home, here I was again: face-to-face with the evil green golf balls.

I was starting to perform the Ritual of Retch. The woof warning was loud. The gack dance had begun.

And then, there was a gentle hand on my arm.

I looked down, and there I saw Penny. She was smiling encouragingly at me. Also, she was leaning her head away whenever I pointed my mouth in her general direction, but I had to expect that.

"Ice cream," she said.

I nodded and set my jaw as bravely as I could.

"It's all just ice cream," I agreed.

I kept repeating it over and over as they loaded my tray with tuna and green noodle casserole. It was ice cream! It didn't look like snot with peas, it looked like ice cream!

And when they loaded on the deep-fried cheese sticks that had popped open and blown their gooey white insides out, I tried *not* to think that they looked like popped zits. They were ice cream!

And even when the dreaded brussels sprouts were loaded up, I just gritted my teeth and chanted the words over and over in my head, *Ice cream, ice cream, ice cream.*

Penny and I found a place to sit. All the kids who'd been on the bus sat as far from me as they could get, except for Penny. There were some other kids, though, who had come from somewhere else and didn't know yet about the bus barfathon. They sat next to us, not knowing the danger they were in.

They did stare just a little, though, when I did what Penny had told me to do. I guess seeing me close my eyes and pinch my nose shut with my free hand seemed slightly strange. I noticed conversation kind of dropped off after that.

I took a forkful of the noodle goo. Not easy to do with your eyes shut. And with shaking hand I put it in my mouth.

Ice cream!

I swallowed. It was amazing! With my eyes and nose closed it *did* kind of seem like ice cream. If ice cream was warm. But I had enough imagination to deal with that little problem. So, it was warm ice cream. So what?

Then came the fried cheese.

Ice cream on a stick, that's what I told myself. And I swallowed it right down. Not one, but several. Half a dozen deep-fried ice creams! And then more of the tuna noodle ice cream! It was working. It was WORKING!

What a moment of pleasure that was.

But pleasure is fleeting, they say. I should have remembered that.

I was ready to try the impossible. I was going to try and gag down a brussels sprout.

Ice cream, ice cream, ice cream.

I poked a fork into the dense little cabbage.

I popped it into my mouth.

It was ice cream!

"What are you doing, you moron?"

I opened my eyes. It was Dreezer. He was looking down at me like he couldn't believe what he was seeing. Hedley and his friends were standing back a ways. I was sure Hedley was responsible for Dreezer noticing me.

I quickly shut my eyes again. If I *saw* those sprouts, I knew the terrible memory would come over me again.

"He's trying to eat," Penny said, speaking for me.

"Well, he has to open his eyes and stop holding his nose," Dreezer said. "It's making people stare."

"He can't," Penny said urgently.

"He *can* and he *will*," Dreezer said. "Mess with the Dreeze, and you get the squeeze," he warned. "Now open your eyes!"

I shook my head no.

"Ice cream, ice cream, ice cream," I muttered. Then, for the first time in years, I forced myself to swallow the sprout.

"Okay, that does it," Dreezer said. "I warned you. I warned you you'd get the squeeze!"

At last I opened my eyes.

Bad timing.

Dreezer was standing over me now, very close. I looked up into that oatmeal and strawberry jam face.

And then he showed me what he meant when he said "Mess with the Dreeze, and you get the squeeze."

As I watched in helpless horror Dreezer raised his hand to his face. Then, with his two index fingers, he selected an especially swollen zit.

I swear it actually made a sound. *Spoink!*

"Ice cream, ice c-c-c-rreeeeam!" I moaned.

But there was no way to pretend it was ice cream.

The zit erupted. It spewed.

Now I knew true terror.

FIVE

By now you know enough about me to guess what happened when Dreezer gave me the squeeze.

Even a normal person might have lost his lunch at the sight of that erupting pustule. And let's face it—I was a long way from being normal.

It was very unfortunate timing, you see, because I had just eaten. I'd eaten that gooey noodle stuff. I'd eaten the fried cheese sticks. I'd even swallowed the one brussels sprout.

I was full. The vomit cannon was loaded. The barf bomb was ready to drop. The puke nuke was ready to be exploded.

"*G-g-g-g-o-v-v-v-bleeaaah!*"

Worse yet, I was loaded with half-digested

food. It hadn't had time yet to liquefy. It was not, shall we say, creamy style. This was chunky. This was extra chunky.

This was rocky road.

You could still recognize the individual cheese sticks as they flew out of my mouth. I must have swallowed one of them whole, because it went twirling through the air like a baton.

"*G-g-ahgg-g-o-vbub-v-bleeaaah!*"

Penny must have seen it coming. She jumped back like a cat being chased by a vacuum cleaner.

But Dreezer was unprepared for my reverse digestion. Dreezer thought he could gross me out and not suffer any consequences.

Ha!

I had hawked up the cheese sticks. I had bubbled over with the noodle mucilage. I still had not fired that brussels sprout.

The last thing down was also the last thing up. I guess you wouldn't think it would work that way. But the process of digestion is truly miraculous. Disgusting but miraculous.

It was like some nightmare replay of the meal with Pastor and Mrs. Roberson. With a throat-scraping, squeezing, pig-through-apython feeling, the brussels sprout reappeared.

But it didn't come shooting out at maximum velocity. It was more like a softball pitch. Or maybe like one of those tennis balls that gets hit way high in the air. A lob, that's what they call it.

It flew. It achieved altitude. Then it just sort of seemed to hang there. Almost like it was levitating in midair.

Dreezer made the mistake of looking up. When he looked up, his mouth opened.

That was his second mistake.

The sprout flew through the air. It trailed a sticky gravy of the noodle stuff like a comet. It plopped down in Dreezer's open mouth.

For about a minute, time just stood still.

It was like nothing moved. No one breathed. Not a sound was heard. The world stopped turning on its axis.

Then Dreezer spit the brussels sprout out.

"You're DEAD!" Dreezer screamed.

I ran. I mean, it wasn't like there was much I could say to make him happy.

I ran. But not back to the cabin, because I knew he'd look for me there.

Instead I ran into the woods, weeping and

gagging and wailing and wishing I had never been born.

Only once I was in the woods, I became terrified. There were wolves in the woods! And poison ivy! And ticks!

I started to run back toward the camp, but I knew Dreezer and Hedley would be waiting for me.

"Why me?" I cried aloud. "Why? Why?"

Fortunately no one answered. That would have scared me to death. I collapsed against a tree trunk. I was sobbing. I had infuriated Dreezer. I had grossed Penny out all over again.

My life was really not going well.

Just then I saw it. At least I thought I saw something. It was flitting between the tree trunks. It moved silently, but it seemed to me that it was very large.

Was it Dreezer? No. It was too large to be Dreezer. And way too large to be Hedley. It looked like a man, and yet . . . there was something weird about it.

It stopped moving. I couldn't see anything but a large shadow. But I knew that shadow was staring at me.

I guess I should have investigated. Or called out and said, "Hey, who's there?"

Instead I said, "W-WAAAAAHH!"

Yes, I screamed like a baby. I screamed in a high, shrill voice like a girl's. Every hair on my head was standing on end. My knees shook. My teeth chattered.

I was faced with a terrible choice: what was scarier? Dreezer and Hedley and a camp full of people who hated me? Or the woods, haunted by some large, weird apparition?

But I couldn't choose. So I just ran, squealing like a pig who's just figured out how they make bacon. I ran in blind terror.

I say *blind* terror because I closed my eyes as I ran.

So I didn't get far.

THONK!

I slammed into a tree at full speed.

The lights went out.

When I came to, it was raining just a little. And Penny was standing over me. I looked up into her pretty face. Her eyes were kind. Her voice was soothing.

"Are you okay?" she asked me.

I blinked. It took me a few seconds to remember what had happened.

Oh, right: ice cream, Dreezer popping his

zit, the brussels sprout flying out of my mouth and into his, running through the woods, the dark shadow staring at me . . .

I was in the woods. Lying on the ground in the woods.

I jumped straight up.

"Ticks!" I yelled. "Ticks! Bloodsucking ticks!"

I tore off my shirt and frantically began searching my skin. I expected at any moment to find one of the little monsters swelling up from sucking my blood.

"In my hair! Check my head!" I begged Penny.

"You *are* pathetic, aren't you?" Penny said.

Her words should have hurt my feelings. But I was busy scratching viciously at my head and yelling, "Ticks! They get on you in the woods. I know they're on me! Help me look, pleeaase!"

"Good grief, Robert," Penny said. "Stop whimpering and I'll look." She grabbed my head and started running her fingers through my hair. "There are no ticks," she announced.

"Maybe the rain kept them off me," I said. I still felt itchy all over. I put my shirt back on, but then I rolled up my pants to check my legs.

"What is the matter with you?" Penny asked. "I've never seen anyone who was such a mess. All you ever do is throw up and squeal. It's like nausea and terror are all you know. Why would you go to summer camp if you're scared of ticks?"

"I didn't want to come to camp," I wailed. "My parents made me."

Penny rolled her eyes. "Why am I not surprised?"

"I just wanted to stay home," I said. The rain was falling harder now. It had soaked my hair and my clothes.

"Come on." Penny took my hand. "We'd better get somewhere and dry off."

"I can't go back to the camp," I said, making a little whinnying noise like a skittish horse. "Dreezer and Hedley . . . they're waiting for me."

"Look, Robert," Penny said, firmly pulling me after her, "sooner or later you'll have to face Dreezer and Hedley. And sooner or later you'll have to stand up to them. Just like sooner or later you'll have to learn to eat brussels sprouts and cheese and even yogurt without gacking up your appendix."

The very thought of Dreezer, Hedley,

brussels sprouts, cheese, and yogurt all together . . .

"Don't you *dare* heave," Penny snapped.

"There was . . . just before I ran into the tree, I thought I saw someone. Or some*thing* watching me," I said. "It was large, maybe like a really big man—I can't be sure."

I expected Penny to tell me I was imagining things. But she stopped walking and looked at me.

"What did it look like?" she asked.

"I told you: I didn't see it clearly. It just looked big and dark."

To my amazement, a look of fear passed across Penny's face.

"Aaaah! What is it?" I cried. "What what what what?"

"Nothing," Penny said, and started to lead us back toward camp again.

"You can't just say it was nothing. I saw your eyes! You were afraid! Trust me, I know fear when I see it."

"I'm telling you, it was nothing," Penny said. "Nothing at all. Let's just head back to camp."

But as she walked she kept checking back over her shoulder.

SIX

I dragged back to the camp, expecting the worst. To my relief, Dreezer wasn't around. But Hedley and his pals were waiting when I went into the cabin. They were lounging in their specially made-up beds, watching their TV with the sound low so no one else could enjoy it.

"Well, well," Hedley said. "If it isn't Baby Worm."

"Baby Worm. Ga-hunh, ga-hunh," Jamal said.

Buttfire was too busy to notice me. He was using a pocket knife to scrape his toe jam.

I went to my bunk and lay down. I was exhausted and depressed and wet. And hungry.

"That was quite a show you put on in the

dining hall," Hedley said. "Mr. Brill had to have Dreezer restrained. He was yelling and grinding his teeth and telling everyone that he was going to kill you."

Going to *kill* me? That was kind of harsh, wasn't it? All I did was puke up a sprout that landed in his mouth. My knees began shaking.

"But don't worry," Hedley said. He got up and came closer. He sat down on the cot across from mine. "Don't you worry about old Dreezer. He isn't going to kill you. I told him that would be wrong."

I looked at Hedley suspiciously. Naturally I didn't believe him. Like I said: I may be a weak-stomached coward, but I'm not an idiot.

Hedley grinned his evil-fat-baby smile. "I see by your expression that you doubt me. But I'm telling you the truth. See, I explained to Dreezer what a hopeless, pathetic wimp you are. And then I pointed out that just killing you would be letting you off easy. No, no, no. It would be much more fun to make your time here at camp into a living nightmare."

"It's already a living nightmare," I said.

Hedley looked disappointed. "Okay, then

Dreezer and I and Jamal and Buttfire are going to combine to make your life a . . . a . . . living hell!"

"It's already a living hell," I said.

Hedley furrowed his brow. "Yeah? Well, we'll make it a worse living hell. We'll make it the worst living hell anyone's ever seen. Ha!"

"Ga-hunh," Jamal added, coming to his master's aid.

But strangely enough, I wasn't totally terrified right then. Oh, sure, my teeth were chattering and my knees were knocking, but my bowels hadn't loosened, and the fear funk that led to panic puking hadn't hit me.

Maybe I was just too tired to work up a really good terror. Maybe that was it. Or maybe I was just distracted. Because even while Hedley was trying to come up with ever more horrifying descriptions of what he was going to do to me, I just kept seeing that large, dark shape in my head.

For dinner they served two things I could actually eat without getting sick: bread and apples. I liked bread, as long as there's no butter. And I could eat apples, as long as I cut them up into tiny pieces so I could be sure there weren't any worms in them.

They also served sloppy joes, but no way was I eating any of that. So I just loaded up on apples and bread. It was kind of nice, actually. I mean, I had a lot of room to myself since only Penny would sit anywhere near me.

After dinner, when it got dark, they made us all go outside. We sat in a big circle on the ground, and they built a bonfire. Then Mr. Brill gave a little speech about how great the camp was and how we were going to have a lot of fun.

I saw Dreezer sitting with Hedley and his pals across the circle. The way it was, I kind of saw them through the fire. The flickering orange glow gave their faces an especially cruel look.

We all sang some songs. It was kind of nice. I figured the fire would keep mosquitoes and ticks away. And the fact that everyone was there together would keep Dreezer and Hedley from being able to do anything to me. Sure, none of the kids except Penny would sit anywhere near me, but that was okay. I was used to that.

"Would you like to roast some marshmal-lows?" Penny asked me.

"NO! NO!" I said.

Penny jumped.

"I mean, no thank you, Penny," I said. "They . . . they make me sick."

"Marshmallows?" she asked. "Marshmallows make you sick?"

I nodded. "Haven't you ever noticed how when you touch a raw marshmallow, it feels almost like skin? Like fat? And then what about when they catch fire and they get all black and the goo is oozing and getting crisp and—"

"Okay, okay," Penny said quickly. "Let it go. Ice cream, think ice cream."

I gritted my teeth. "Don't say ice cream," I groaned. "Ever since lunch, anytime I think about ice cream, I see cheese sticks and b-b-b-"

"Brussels sprouts?"

I jumped up and ran away from the fire. I decorated several bushes with my barf, then came back to Penny.

"I don't know how much more of you I can stand," Penny said sadly.

I nodded. "I understand. If you want to go

sit somewhere else, that would be okay. I never keep friends for long."

"You have got to get your act together, Robert," she said.

Just then the counselors started shushing everybody. Everyone fell silent.

Then Mr. Brill stood up.

"He's going to tell a story," Penny whispered to me. "A scary story."

"How do you know?" I asked.

"They do it every year. They tell of the terrible legend in the woods. One of the other kids told me. Maybe you'd better leave."

I was a little stung by the way she said that. Like she just assumed I would be scared. Okay, I *was* already getting up to go to the cabin. But I was hurt by the scorn in Penny's voice. So I sat back down. Just to show her.

"I'm going to tell you a tale," Mr. Brill began. "But this isn't just some ghost story. No, children, this is far more than a ghost story. This . . . is the legend of Bigfart!"

"Bigfoot?" I whispered to Penny.

"No," she said. "Big*fart*."

"This is a joke, right?" I said. But Penny just looked at me and shook her head slowly.

Mr. Brill waited till everyone was quiet. "First off, let me make one thing clear: this is no tall tale. What I'm about to tell you is true, even though they say it's a legend.

"Now, you've all heard of Big*foot*. He's the monster that lives deep in the woods and is rarely seen. Well, Big*fart* is Bigfoot's bigger brother. And unlike Bigfoot, who is actually rather shy, Bigfart is a truly dangerous creature. Truly dangerous."

He looked around the circle at us.

"Some say Bigfart looks like a man. Some say he looks more like a gorilla. Others say he's the last of a dying breed of prehistoric half men, half apes. One thing is for sure: he lives in these very woods."

Mr. Brill swung his arm around at the trees that hemmed in all around us.

I scooted closer to the fire. A terrible thought had just begun to seep into my brain: that dark figure I'd seen in the woods. Could it be . . . ?

"Yes, in these very woods!" Mr. Brill said loudly. "And every year he appears to one unlucky camper. Only one."

Okay, now this was starting to worry me. I could feel a creepy, crawly feeling on the back of my neck. It was either the hairs standing on end or ticks crawling up my neck looking for a place to suck blood directly from my brain.

Either way, I wanted no more of this. But what was I going to do? Leave the fire and all the rest of the kids and walk back to a dark empty cabin where, for all I knew, Bigfart was waiting for me?

"Why do they call him Bigfart?" Hedley asked. He gave me a wink, like he was saying, "Hey, listen to *this*, Baby Worm."

Mr. Brill nodded cordially to Hedley and sent him a greasy smile. "They call him Bigfart because that's how he destroys his victims. See, kids, Bigfart is an unusual creature. All year long he eats. He eats whatever he can find. He eats the maggots in garbage. He eats the termites in rotting logs. He eats the beetles that scurry beneath the moldering leaves. He eats the leftovers of dead possums and dead skunks, whatever's left behind after the wolves are done with them. And all year long he just eats and never goes. Eats every kind of disgusting food and never, ever *goes*. Never even lets go of a whiff of gas because he's saving it up, see. Saving every ounce of stench. Saving it all for one horrible, gigantic, monster FART!"

That was too much. My stomach had started doing the gack dance from the moment Brill had said the word *maggots*. The countdown had started.

Ten . . . nine . . .

"Get back," I told Penny through gritted teeth.

Penny didn't have to be warned twice. She moved away to a safe distance.

"They don't call him Bigfart for nothing!" Mr. Brill went on. "He farts only once per year. He chooses one victim, one unlucky camper, and hits him full blast with the buttal explosion to end all buttal explosions. We're talking a force-ten farticane."

Eight . . . seven . . .

My head was swimming. I was halfway through the countdown to a pukelear explosion in the megachunk range. But at the same time I was too terrified to move. My legs had turned to overcooked spaghetti.

And still Mr. Brill went on. His voice was weird. There was an insane edge to it.

Six . . . five . . .

The gack dance was under way. The backup singers of barf were performing the vocals of vomit in my throat.

"One poor victim each year," he repeated. "The first kid to encounter Bigfart was nine years old. But after he experienced Bigfart's stench, he was aged seventy years instantly! His hair turned gray, his teeth fell out, and he could no longer stand loud music."

Four . . . three . . .

"One girl who was victimized by Bigfart's fart *had* been a genius. She was left unable to add, subtract, or even comb her hair. All she could do was stare into space and say, 'Could you please open the window?' over and over and over."

Two . . . one . . .

"One boy who suffered Bigfart's attack was actually turned into a girl! You see, no one who encounters Bigfart is ever left unchanged!" Mr. Brill's face glowed yellow and red from the firelight. His eyes were bright as he stared at each of us in turn. "You have no idea of the awesome power of that maggot, termite, rotting meat, saved-up-for-a-year fart! No idea!"

I had an idea of the power of such a fart. I had a very good imagination when it came to disgusting things. I tried to get up, but my legs gave way. The only thing that worked was my stomach.

It was working all too well.

Zero!

"*Huff-huff-hug-g-g-hug-gag-gaw-BLEAH!*"

I did the blew magoo. I huffed into my own lap.

"Ha, ha, I knew he'd heave!" Hedley cried gleefully. "You all think Bigfart is something to worry about? The real danger is Baby Worm! Once you've been magooed by Baby Worm, you're never the same!"

"Let's get him!" Dreezer said, jumping to his feet.

"You'd better get out of here," Penny urged me.

But by then I was up and running. I raced toward the cabin.

I knew what was happening. The story of Bigfart had scared the kids, at least a little. And now Hedley and Dreezer had turned that fear against me.

I ran for the cabin. I didn't know where else to go.

I tore through the door. I didn't have any plan. I just wanted to crawl under the covers, even though I was covered with chunkage, and hope everyone would leave me alone.

I threw back the covers. I leapt into the bed. BAM!

The bed collapsed under me. I fell right through it.

BAM!

I hit the floor. The floorboards fell away.

BAM!

I hit the ground under the cabin. I landed in something soft and mushy and aromatic.

It smelled like ordure. Horse manure, to be exact.

Dreezer, Hedley, Jamal, and Buttfire were all crowded around peering down at me. They were laughing. Laughing and laughing and laughing. They had cut the bottom of my bunk away. And then they had sawed through the floor of the cabin.

"That was excellent," Dreezer complimented Hedley. "That got him *good*. It worked just the way you said it would."

"Now you see why you shouldn't kill him? Just think," Hedley said, "camp has only begun. We have two whole weeks to humiliate him!"

SEVEN

Fortunately there was a spare cot, so I had a place to sleep that night.

I guess by now you think I was a pretty lame excuse for a human being, right? You'd be right. I was.

A pathetic, puking coward. That's what I was. And every time I thought I had sunk as low as I could sink, I sank lower still.

Lots of kids don't like summer camp all that much. But I think it's safe to say that my camp experience was the worst camp experience in the entire history of camps.

And it was just getting worse.

The next day they made us go canoeing. I don't know why. It's just one of those things you have to do at summer camp.

I ran into Penny again when they were marching us all down to the edge of the lake.

"They're going to make us go out on the water, aren't they?" I whimpered.

"Let me guess: you're afraid of the water, right?"

"No, I'm not afraid of water," I said huffily. "There's nothing wrong with *water*. It's drowning I'm afraid of. Slipping below the surface, gasping for air. Air! Air! Give me air! Sinking lower and lower till you're on the bottom, tangled in the seaweed. Suffocating!"

Penny shook her head. "You're a real piece of work, aren't you? Look, at least out on the lake Dreezer and Hedley can't get to you."

"That's what you think," I said darkly.

"And there are no ticks out on the lake."

"Maybe some got in the canoe and are waiting for me," I said.

"As far as we know, Bigfart can't swim," Penny said.

"I guess that's true," I admitted.

"And see, if you stay behind onshore, you'll be all alone in the camp. All alone, with Bigfart right out there in the woods."

"Oh. Oh, you're right!" I cried. "If I go, I could drown. If I stay, I'd be alone—no one but me and . . . and . . . Bigfart."

Penny was looking thoughtfully at me. "Just out of curiosity, how do you handle it when you're stuck between two things you're scared of?"

I shrugged. "Usually I just run crying to my parents. But they aren't here."

"So you have to decide which is worse— going with me in the canoe or waiting here in camp for Bigfart." She smiled. "Come on, Robert. Come canoeing with me. I won't let you drown."

The way she said it was so sweet and so confident that I almost decided to be brave and go with her.

Almost.

What I actually did was just sit down and cry and weep and howl till Mr. Brill had two of the counselors pick me up and throw me into the canoe like a sack of potatoes.

Once in the canoe I lay in the bottom, clutching my life jacket around me. Penny took care of paddling. I begged her not to paddle out too far. But I don't know if she did or not, because I never looked.

"Robert, let me ask you a question," Penny said. "You told me the story of the brussels sprout, the dentures, and the wig. So I know when you realized you had a weak stomach. But when did you realize you were such a . . . well, such a coward? I mean, no offense, but the average rabbit is braver than you."

"When did I first discover that I had no courage?" I asked bitterly. "It was a long time ago, Penny. I was just a little kid at the time. But still, it's something I'll never forget. It happened one night. One terrible night."

I remember that my mom had run out to the store to get some groceries or something. It was Christmas Eve, so maybe she had to get some last-minute cranberry sauce. Anyway, I was home with my dad and my little sister, Jennifer, who was still a baby back then. We had a fire going in the fireplace. There was a big bowl of eggnog out on the table. The Christmas tree was lit up and beautiful. Our cat, Babs, was dozing on the mantel.

It was a perfect night.

Then the phone rang. It was for my dad. It was some kind of alert for the Marine base and he had to leave right away. He was a little worried because my mom wasn't home, and I wasn't really old enough to be left alone with the baby.

But he had no choice. He's a Marine and Marines take orders. Besides, we figured my mom would be home any minute.

I said, "It's okay, Dad. I can take care of everything. Don't you worry. I'm not afraid!"

I think that was the last time in my life that I ever said "I'm not afraid."

It was creepy being all alone in the house. But I was trying to be brave, trying not to be scared. Then things started to go wrong.

First Jennifer started crying. When I went over to her crib to find out why, I realized the answer: there was the definite stench of baby product. I didn't want to change her diaper, but she wouldn't stop yelling.

So I did it. I opened up her Pampers diaper and came face to face with the deadly, yellow-brown diaper gravy.

Just then there was a knock at the door. I jumped, startled. I hesitated: I knew I shouldn't answer the door. Besides, Jennifer's reeking diaper was still open.

But I told myself not to be a coward. I went to the door. It was a kid from across the street. A kid I knew.

I opened the door. I saw that he had his dog with him. His dog's name was Psycho. It was the perfect name for this dog, trust me.

"Hi," I said.

"Hi," he said back. "Look, my dad sent me over to borrow your dad's power drill. He's doing something with the Christmas lights."

"I guess that's okay," I said. "Come in. But you'd better leave Psycho outside."

"What? You're afraid of my dog?"

"I didn't say I was afraid. It's just that you know how he gets sometimes."

"Little Bobby, afraid of a dog," he taunted me. "What are you, a baby?"

Well, in those days, before I knew that I was doomed to be a coward for life, I used to get upset when people would call me names.

"Your dog doesn't scare me," I sneered. I held open the door. The boy and his dog stepped inside.

It all happened so quickly.

Babs the cat took one look at Psycho. Babs's tail got big and the hair on her back stood up.

Psycho growled. Babs hissed. Psycho attacked. Babs jumped. Right onto the table.

Psycho went after her.

"NO!" I cried, but it was too late. The huge

bowl of eggnog shattered. The viscous yellow goo drenched Babs and Psycho.

Now they were screaming around the room like they each had been strapped to a rocket. *Zoom! Zoom! Raww-rawwr-rawwr! Meo-OWWWW! RUFF-RFUFF-RFUFF! Zoom! MerrrOWWW!*

And wherever they went, they spread the eggnog. Over the couch. Over the walls. Over the presents under the tree.

"STOP!" I kept yelling. "Help me get them!" I demanded of the kid from across the street. But he wouldn't. He just laughed.

Then Babs leapt right over Jennifer. Psycho came after Babs. But you know how dogs are. They love anything that stinks.

And few things stink like diaper gravy.

Psycho grabbed Jennifer's full diaper in his teeth. And he kept after Babs.

Eggnog and diaper gravy flew everywhere! Brown streaks across the wallpaper. Little dripping baby chunks filled the air, like we were caught in a blender loaded with poop, eggs, cream, and a little brandy.

I cried out for help. A brown drop landed on my tongue.

I screamed. I felt my stomach heaving.

Just then Babs made one last, desperate leap. *MEERowwrOWWW!* And landed on the Christmas tree.

Down, down came the Christmas tree! I ran to catch it. The needles stuck me and I cried out. But when I closed my mouth, my teeth bit right through a string of Christmas lights.

If you've never had your teeth electrocuted, let me give you a little clue: IT HURTS!

The force of the jolt knocked me on my butt. I was jerking and spazzing, out of control. My stomach had already started to do the gack dance before I got shocked, and now it just let loose.

But it wasn't just my stomach that lost control. I blew. I squirted. I dumped. All at the same time. It was a simultaneous explosion of bodily functions.

That's how my mom found me when she got home. I was sitting on the floor, stinking, in a puddle of sewage. The entire room had been destroyed. There was baby ordure everywhere, mixed with eggnog. The presents were crushed. The tree had fallen. Jennifer was screaming.

Of course Psycho and his owner were gone by then. The kid never even admitted he'd been responsible.

Christmas was definitely messed up. So was I. After that I was scared of dogs, cats, babies, diapers, eggs, cream, pine trees, electricity, colored lights, being alone, answering the door, and the kid from across the street. Since then I've just kept adding to the list of things that terrify me.

One thing was for sure: I never tried to be brave again.

When I was done telling my sad story, Penny looked down at me, cowering in the bottom of the canoe. Her eyes were filled with pity. Or contempt. It's hard to tell those two emotions apart. She said, "And who was the kid from across the street?"

She had guessed the answer of course.

"Hedley," I said bitterly. "Hedley Hampton."

"There he is now," Penny said.

"Where?"

"He's in a canoe with those two jerks of his. They're coming closer."

Summoning up all my courage, I peeked over the edge of the boat. Sure enough, Hedley, Jamal, and Buttfire were drawing near.

"There he is!" Jamal cried out. "Ga-hunh, ga-hunh."

"Hey, Robert," Hedley yelled. "Bobby! Buttfire here has a little present for you."

I was already shaking. Now I started to rattle. "W-w-w-what?"

Hedley pointed to Buttfire. Buttfire was holding a pillowcase. Something seemed to be squirming around inside the pillowcase. Something alive.

"He's got a pet for you, Bobby," Hedley said gleefully. "Tell Bobby what you have for him, Buttfire."

"Um, what?" Buttfire said.

Hedley rolled his eyes. "It's a skunk, Baby Worm. And it's all yours! Let fly, Buttfire!"

Buttfire drew back his arm. Then he launched the pillowcase through the air.

In midair you could see it turning. Turning and squirming as it flew toward us.

"Jump!" Penny screamed. "Robert, jump!"

She followed her own advice and dived over the side. She was safely underwater when the skunk hit.

It landed in the bottom of the canoe, just inches from me.

The skunk emerged from the pillowcase. It made an angry chittering noise at me. Then it turned around and took aim.

I made a desperate grab for the skunk, hoping to throw it over the side.

Just as I grabbed on, the skunk fired.

"AAAAAARRRRRGGGHHHH!" I screamed, and dropped the skunk. The skunk fired again.

The smell . . . the horror of that smell. It was everywhere! It was all over me! The entire world was nothing but that horrible smell.

"Ha-HAAA! That was *perfect*!" Hedley crowed.

"Ga-hunh, ga-hunh, ga-hunh," Jamal laughed.

"Oh, Robert, blub, blub," Penny moaned from the water nearby. "You should have jumped."

"He couldn't," Hedley sneered. "Baby Worm is scared of the water. Baby Worm is scared of everything."

EIGHT

"Wake up, you reeking, stinking, disgusting, spineless vomit bag."

It was Dreezer. He was kicking the legs of my cot. I had slept right through the alarm. Probably because I hadn't really been able to fall asleep till almost dawn.

The skunk stench still clung to me. I'd taken a shower the night before. I'd scrubbed my hair with strong soap. Nothing had worked. I still reeked of skunk. I had spent the night trying to hold my nose so I wouldn't smell myself. It didn't work. And every time I smelled myself, I had to run to the outhouse to do the old kneel and spew. By about four in the morning I think I finally gagged up my liver.

Not a great night. And morning didn't look like any kind of improvement.

"Get up, you creep," Dreezer said. "I'd drag you out of bed, but that would mean touching you. And I ain't getting any of that stench on me."

"I'm awake, I'm awake," I said.

"It's horseback riding day," Dreezer said. "Although I pity the poor horse who has to carry you."

"I don't want to ride any horses," I moaned.

"Tough. You have to go. Mr. Brill says everyone goes."

Well, I guess by now you won't be totally surprised if I tell you that I was scared of horses. The very idea of getting on top of one was enough to make me go stiff with terror. But I knew I was doomed. I knew I'd end up having to go. So I decided just to accept it. To take it like a man.

Okay, that last part is a lie. They had to drag me out, whimpering and whining and crying. But in my mind I was accepting. I won't bore you with the story of that horse ride. I think you can imagine how I handled it. The most exciting part was when I got motion sick and magooed all over the horse and he bucked me off into a tree and red ants climbed all over me and bit me while I screamed and ran around tearing my clothes off and begging everyone to let me go home.

You know, the usual.

But what was *not* usual about the trip was the fact that Hedley, Jamal, and Buttfire weren't there. Neither was Dreezer. None of my tormentors had come along. All had stayed back in the camp. Not that the rest of the people were exactly my friends. Let's face it: all of them hated me. All except Penny. And even she kind of kept her distance because of the lingering skunk stench.

Still, as nice as it was not to have Hedley around, it kind of worried me, too. Dreezer had been so pushy about me going on the ride. He had to be up to something.

Eventually we returned to the camp. There were Hedley and all the rest of them. They were acting very strangely. For one thing, all through dinner none of them even said anything to me.

This just made me more suspicious. I knew something was up. I just didn't know what.

It didn't happen until after dinner. I was feeling kind of good because at dinner we'd had mashed potatoes and chicken. I can eat chicken as long as it doesn't have any skin on it or any bones. And as long as I don't find one of those veins in it. You know how sometimes you're biting into a piece of chicken and you see this little bluish blood vessel? Well, that's guaranteed to make me launch on sight. But as long as nothing like that happens, I like chicken.

So anyway, the skunk smell was mostly gone by dinnertime. And the pain of the ant stings had gone down after I smeared my entire body with pink lotion. And I hadn't lost any of my dinner . . . yet. Plus, I was starting to hope that maybe, just maybe Hedley and Dreezer had gotten tired of torturing me.

I was relaxing on my cot when disaster struck.

"Hey, what's this?" Buttfire asked Hedley in a loud voice.

"What are you talking about?" Hedley said.

"I've got something in my armpit," Buttfire said.

"Why, whatever could it be?"

"I don't know," Buttfire said. "What's it look like?"

"I can't see," Hedley said. "My eyesight isn't

80

too good. But do you know who has great eye-sight? Our friend Robert. Hey, Robert, come over here and take a look at Buttfire's armpit."

The thought of Buttfire's armpit made me want to chunkulate. And since I'm not an idiot, I *knew* I was being set up. But what was I supposed to do?

"Get over here, Robert," Hedley said. "Get over here and take a close look at Buttfire's pit."

Feeling like a condemned man on his way to the firing squad, I got up. I walked down that long aisle. Waiting for me: Hedley, Jamal, and Buttfire. Just then I felt someone's eyes on my back. I glanced over my shoulder. Sure enough: Dreezer was standing in the doorway to the cabin, leering and grinning.

I started to whimper, just a little. But I marched on, afraid to disobey.

"Show him, Buttfire," Hedley said in a dangerous whisper.

Buttfire raised his arm. He shoved his pit close to my nose. That was bad enough. But the real horror sat in the middle of Buttfire's smelly pit: a fat, swollen, bloodsucking tick.

At that very moment Buttfire reached up and squeezed the tick. It popped! Its spidery, swollen body burst open!

I screamed.

I ran for the outhouse.

I was about to get another look at all that mashed potatoes and skin-free, no-vein chicken.

I raced into the night. There was a storm just starting to break. Lightning flashed. Thunder rumbled. I threw open the outhouse door. I dropped to my knees before the reeking wooden seat.

And then . . . the seat just gave way.

I pitched forward into the darkness.

I clawed desperately, trying not to fall in.

Below me was the pool of sewage. The collected crud of a camp full of kids.

My hands scrabbled helplessly. But down I fell. Down, and down, and down.

I landed with a gurgling splash.

I sank in ripe ordure up to my neck.

To this day, I can't tell you how I made it out of that outhouse septic tank. My memory of it has faded away. I'm grateful for that.

The next thing I remembered, I was staggering through the woods. Staggering through the woods covered with brown substance. I guess I was delirious. I guess I was hysterical. I know for a fact that I didn't look too good.

The woods were dark, but I was beyond normal fear. Besides, now the lightning was exploding in the sky above me, and I was scared of lightning.

I staggered and wept, and staggered and boohooed, and cursed my fate. The rain began to fall. But this wasn't all bad. It washed some of the worst of the doo stew from me.

Then I saw a light.

It was a warm, yellow light, deep in the woods. Normally I would have scampered away. But I was running out of choices, you know? What was I going to do? Go back to the camp? Stay in the woods forever?

I went toward the light. It came from a window. The window was in a simple log cabin.

Weeping and hopeless, I found a door.

"H-h-h-hello, is anyone h-h-h-home?" I called out.

There was no answer. I opened the door and went in.

There was a warm, cheerful fire going in the fireplace. There was a couch, piled with little pillows. There was an inviting feather bed. It was like someplace out of a fairy tale. It was like those pictures of the house where Red Riding Hood's granny lives.

It gave me a warm, safe feeling just being there. I collapsed in a chair by the fireplace. I felt incredibly weary. And as the thunder crashed outside I closed my eyes and drifted off into sleep.

In my sleep I dreamed I was still back there in that septic ooze. Still flailing around and cursing my life. I dreamed of every time I had been humiliated by my weak stomach and weaker courage. It all came swimming back up to me, like floaters in a toilet bowl. I saw it all: the terrible dinner with Pastor Roberson and his wife, the Christmas baby poop and eggnog disaster, the day Hedley sent me toilet diving into that buttwurst, and all the other times. So many of them. Throwing up all over the wedding cake at my aunt's wedding. And doing the same thing when she got married again. And the third time she got married, how she didn't even have a cake, but I huffed up during the ceremony itself all over the flower girl, who then blew chunks onto the best man, which set off a chain reaction of universal hufferage that ended with the bride and groom committing face-to-face magoo at the very moment they were supposed to kiss.

There was a lot to remember. It was a long flashback.

I woke slowly, dreamily, to see a woman who looked a little like my grandmother. (Or at least the way I *remember* my grandmother. She's been avoiding me since the day I saw her without her wig or her teeth and I magooed all over her favorite muumuu.)

Anyway, this grandmotherly lady was bending over me and smiling.

I shrank back in alarm.

"Don't be frightened, dear," she said. She smiled.

"I'm s-s-s-sorry I came in," I said. "Don't be mad, okay? I mean, the door was open."

"You're welcome here, my dear," she said. "You look a mess. Why don't you go clean up? Just go through there." She pointed to a door. "You'll find everything you need."

I nodded slowly. She wasn't threatening me, and that was a good thing. Besides, I figured maybe I could sneak out through a window and run away before she tried to hurt me.

I did as she said. I went where she pointed.

It was a bathroom. A perfectly normal bathroom. The only thing odd was that the shower was already running, nice and hot and steamy.

I got undressed and climbed in. The water was the perfect temperature. There were all sorts of shampoos and soaps around. I used all of them.

When I climbed out, I felt a lot better. My clothes, which had been filthy, were hung on the back of the door, clean and ironed. Maybe a little too much starch in the collar, but I could deal with that.

I dressed and went out to see the old lady. She was working at the stove, humming some tune to herself. I suddenly realized I was very hungry. Not surprising, considering that I'd gacked up everything I'd had to eat.

"Oh, there you are, dear," the old woman said. She made a crinkly, wrinkly little smile at me. "Come, have something to eat. You must be famished."

"Well, ma'am, I have this kind of weak stomach. Maybe it's better if I don't—"

"Mashed potatoes," the old woman said, holding up a big spoonful so I could see. "And nice white bread and skinless, boneless, no-vein chicken. And for dessert, ice cream."

It was amazing. It was like my perfect meal. How could she possibly have known?

I was a little suspicious. But at the same time, I was hungry. And my only other choice was going back outside into the rain and thunder and the dark woods where Bigfart lurked.

So I ate. And I ate. And I ate. I don't think I've ever eaten so much in my life. It was like I couldn't stop myself. And as much as I ate, the old lady gave me more.

"What's your name?" the old lady asked.

"Robert Warmack," I said, mumbling through the ice cream.

"You mean Baby Worm, don't you?"

I froze.

Okay, there was no way she could know that. No way.

She smiled at me, but her smile was different somehow.

"All is not what it seems," she said. Only now her voice was very low and slow. It was more like a rumbling growl.

"Ma'am? I think maybe I should go." I was already up and heading for the door.

"You can go, Baby Worm," she said. "But if you go now, you will be Baby Worm forever."

That made me stop. But I didn't turn around. "What do you mean?"

"I mean that you have reached a turning point in your life."

The voice was definitely very low now. Very, very low, like it came from someone very, very big. Not at all like the voice of a sweet little grandmother.

The voice behind me said, "It is time for you to decide. You can face the worst thing in the world. It may destroy you. It may make you a better person. But one thing is certain, Robert Warmack, also known as Baby Worm: if you face this one great test, you will never be the same again."

"W-w-w-w-wha-wha?" I swallowed hard and tried again. "W-w-wha-wha-wha-wha-what do y-y-y-y-you mean?"

"I mean," it growled, "it is time for you to turn around, be a man, and face me. Face . . . BIGFART!"

NINE

"**B**IGFART?" I screamed. "*The* Bigfart?"

"Yes. I am the one known as Bigfart," he said. "The old woman was merely an illusion I created."

I was still facing the door. I hadn't turned around yet. I didn't want to see. I just wanted to leave.

"If you flee now, you will be unchanged," Bigfart said in his Darth Vader voice.

I knew he was right. I knew I should stay and endure the terrible test he planned for me. And I'd like to say that at that moment I reached deep down inside and found the courage I'd lost.

I'd like to say that. But it wouldn't be true. I was outta there!

Or at least, I was trying to be outta there. But my fingers were shaking so badly, I couldn't grasp the doorknob.

"Come on, Robert," I muttered. "Come on, boy, steady now."

But my fingers wouldn't stop shaking. Probably because my whole hands were shaking. And my arms. And the entire rest of my body from my heels to my hair. I was shaking and twitching and jerking and rattling like a squirrel who's been living on coffee beans.

I could not open that door.

It was then that I reached way down deep inside myself and found . . . my basic ability to grovel and beg.

I threw myself down on the floor. "Oh, please, oh please, Mr. Bigfart. PLEEEEEEASE don't destroy me. I don't want to be destroyed. I've never wanted to be destroyed. Being destroyed is against my religion. Don't hurt me. Don't let go of that big one you've been saving up."

"Robert, you must choose: stay or go."

"I'm *trying* to choose. I've chosen. I'm just shaking too badly to open the door."

"Then you have chosen to stay," Bigfart intoned.

"No way—I did not!"

"Did so."

"Did not!"

"Look, kid, the bottom line is: I have to cut one. I've been saving up all year, and I have to let it go. I'm at maximum inflation. This will be Bigfart's biggest fart."

"But why me?" I cried.

"Because you need me. I've been watching you. I've seen what you're like. And I have to tell you, if anyone ever needed the transforming test of Bigfart's deadly gasser, it's you. I mean, come on: you're pathetic."

Okay, it was then that I reached deep down inside and found that tiny, shriveled, almost invisible kernel of courage.

I opened my eyes. And I looked at him.

He was about the size of Shaquille O'Neal. Maybe a little bigger. Only he wasn't bald. In fact, he wasn't bald anywhere on his body. He was as shaggy as a sheepdog.

Actually he was kind of cute in a big, fuzzy sort of way. Cute, that is, until I realized that his fur was *moving*!

His fur was crawling and seething and twisting with every kind of insect known to man, and some no one had ever met before. There were beetles. There were roaches. There were fleas, hopping around him like a mist. There were spiders. There were ticks, swollen and bloated till they were as big as marbles.

Then I looked at his face. His eyes were yellow, like globules of snot rimmed with red. His nose was flat, with nostrils that opened so wide you could see halfway to his brain, like you were looking down a long, hairy tunnel. His mouth and teeth looked like those pictures they show you at the dentist's office to scare you into flossing regularly.

Bigfart didn't floss, from the look of it. If he *had* flossed, he probably wouldn't have had pieces and chunks of filth stuck in the big gaps between his rotting teeth. I stared in horror at that mouth. I stared closely at the things stuck in his teeth.

And the things stuck in his teeth stared right back at me.

Bigfart had been eating bugs.

Then I had a terrible thought. Slowly I turned my gaze toward the table. The table where I had eaten a huge meal just moments before.

The bowls were the same. What was *in* the bowls was different. Oh, yes. Way different.

"WORMS!" I cried. "SLUGS! LEECHES! BUGS!"

"Yes, it is all a part of your test, Robert."

"I ate BUGS!" I screamed.

"You must overcome your weaknesses," Bigfart said solemnly. "This is your greatest test. If you pass, you will be forever changed. You will be free."

"AAAAAAAGGGGHHHHH!" I could picture myself sitting there, deceived by Bigfart's spell, chomping down on worms and crickets and maggots and leeches and brightly colored beetles.

And then I could picture all those creatures still in my stomach.

And then I could picture them all still in my stomach *ALIVE!*

"NOOOOOOOO!" I screamed, clutching at my throat.

"You must not barf!" Bigfart said sternly. "*That* is your test."

Not heave? With a stomach full of living, crawling, squirming insects and worms? Yeah, right. I could picture them down there in my stomach. Right now they would be crying out in their little worm voices as the stomach acid poured in on them. The roaches and crickets would be twitching their antennas, and motoring their little legs, and leaping around trying to avoid the burning liquid.

Some might still be stuck in my esophagus. They were trying desperately to hold on, to avoid being swept down into my stomach. Husband cockroaches were trying to hold on to wife cockroaches.

Hold on! they cried. Don't let go! We'll be safe in the esophagus!

But down in my stomach it would be a nightmare. The burning acid dissolving compound eyes and mandibles. Separating the thoraxes from the abdomens. Eating away the spiny insect hairs. The leeches would pop like water balloons, spilling their load of stale blood.

Perhaps a few brave, intrepid bugs would make a run for it. They would see the opening of the duodenum and cry, This way, everyone! This way!

Their hopes would be dashed because the opening of the duodenum doesn't lead to freedom. No, it leads to the intestines.

"You must not heave!" Bigfart said again. "Not a single extruded chunk may pass your lips!"

But my throat was already doing the gack dance. It was gack dancing like an entire chorus line. I wasn't just going to blow chunks. I was going to urp up all my internal organs!

"No! No, Robert! You must find the strength. You must hold on!"

Just then I realized something. See, if I extruded, it wasn't going to be a guttal explosion of chewed food. No. If I magooed, it was going to be a geyser of half-digested but probably still living worms, leeches, slugs, and assorted bugs.

This did not paint a pretty picture in my mind. It was either bug stew exploding out of my mouth or bug stew slithering sluggishly down my digestive system.

I made a snap decision. I gritted my teeth. I clenched my jaw.

It was bad enough to have a stomach full of bugs and slugs. I didn't need to see them all again.

But it was the most difficult struggle of my life. The gack dance was a whole mosh pit of slam-dancing punk rockers. I mean, my stomach was saying, Here it comes, right back at you, dude!

But I clamped my hands over my mouth

and concentrated with all my might. I could not allow myself to extrude.

"Good," Bigfart said. "You have found your inner strength."

I wanted to say something really sarcastic to him, but opening my mouth would have been a bad idea right then.

"Now it is time to truly put you to the test," Bigfart said.

"MMMMFFFF!" I protested. "MMM-FFF-MMMNNN!"

"I have eaten a hundred pounds or more of everything that creeps or crawls or slithers across the floor of the forest," Bigfart intoned. "I have eaten dead possums and voles and rats and skunks. I have even consumed mushrooms. And I have held it all within my mighty bowels. I have not let even the faintest whiff pass from me. No vapor hath escaped."

This description wasn't really helping my desperate attempt to avoid emitting.

"I have retained it all, every decayed, rotting, maggot-ridden square centimeter of it. I have allowed it all to ripen. To ferment within the putrid folds of my guts. It has aged, like a fine wine. And now . . . NOW it is time to release the vapors of death!"

"NNNNRRRRR," I moaned, still unable to risk opening my mouth. "NNRRRR! NNRRRR!"

Bigfart just looked at me with his pus-yellow eyes and smiled a filthy grin. "I see that you are ready."

I shook my head violently. No, no, no, I wasn't ready. I snapped my head back and forth so hard and so fast, I'm surprised I didn't unscrew my head from my neck.

But Bigfart just kept nodding, like I'd said yes.

You know, I hate to be suspicious, but I think maybe Bigfart just really, really had to cut one, and he didn't care all that much whether I was ready.

"The time has come!" he cried.

He waved his hand and the light went out. We were plunged into darkness. I couldn't see anything.

But that didn't help, because I could still hear.

BOOOOOOM!

The first buttal explosion was like a bomb going off in the room. My ears were ringing. I felt like the floor and walls had rattled.

But it was only the opening salvo of Bigfart's mighty fart attack.

BLAAAAAAAT! BLAAAAAT! BLAAAAT!

Explosion followed explosion, rapid fire. It was the multipopper to end all multipoppers.

POP! POP! POPOPOPOPOPOPOPOP!

Then it turned into a squeezer.

SQQQQUEEEEEEEEEEEEEZE!

It was like an entire orchestra horn section. Like a hundred trumpets playing, and a hundred trombones, and a hundred . . . a hundred whatever horns there are. Tubas! Yes, like a hundred tubas blatting simultaneously.

Then, most terrifying of all, the fart went ninja.

I couldn't hear a thing, but I knew from the way the wind was blowing around the room that he was cutting a silent killer. A ninja fart: the most deadly fart of all.

WWOOOOOSHH!

A tornado had formed in the middle of the room. It twisted violently, fed by the awesome force of Bigfart's flatus. It twisted and the wind tore at me, whipping my hair, blurring my eyes. All the scattered debris in the room, the bowls of bugs and slugs, the furniture, everything went flying!

And then, suddenly, silence fell.

It was the silence of a graveyard.

It was the silence that was total. I knew Bigfart was gone. I knew that I was alone, locked in that room. Alone with Bigfart's most terrible fart.

But so far I had smelled nothing.

Of course that was because I'd been holding my breath. And I knew that wasn't going to last much longer. Sooner or later, I would have to breathe.

My face was red. The sweat poured from me. I was still clutching my mouth, desperately holding on to my stomach load of twisting, squirming horror.

And now, to top it all off, I was trying not to breathe.

And yet I had to breathe.

I flat-out *had* to breathe.

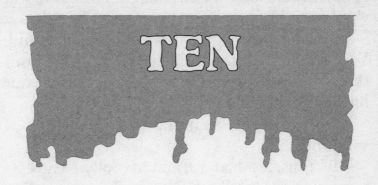

TEN

I breathed.
Through my nose . . . I breathed.

How? How can I even begin to explain what I smelled? There are no words for the nauseating experience that followed.

But I'll try anyway.

I breathed in, and it was as if every stink, reek, stench, odor, foul aroma, miasma, effluvium, fume, fetor, and funk since the beginning of time came together in that one awful whiff.

Add up every fart ever farted by human beings going back to ancient times. Add dog farts. Add pig farts. Add the farts of dinosaurs, who probably really knew how to fart. Add them all together, boil them down till they are concentrated essence of stench. And you still would not have the fart that Bigfart farted.

It wasn't just a gas. It was almost a liquid. You could feel the stench clinging to your skin. You could feel it being sucked down your burning nostrils.

The world was spinning . . . spinning . . . spinning.

My muscles had turned to jelly. My ears were ringing loudly. I felt like I was standing on the railroad tracks in front of a speeding locomotive. It was coming at me, coming at me, COMING AT ME!

The stench hit full force.

It knocked me against the wall. My head was spinning. Where was I? What was happening? I was lost, falling, falling through time and space on a magic carpet of poopfume.

Images rushed before my eyes, like crazy movies of things I'd done and places I'd been. I saw myself hurling for the first time when I was a tiny baby, spewing into my grandma's face. I saw my very first lunch-room extrusion, all over a kid named Joey. I saw it all, every gack dance, every heave, every gut geyser, every time I lost a tooth from the force of the stomach storm. It was like a highlights reel of my lifetime of doing the blew magoo.

Then . . . right then, I knew: it had to stop. It HAD to stop.

Bigfart was right. I had to change. I couldn't keep on the way I'd been going. Someday I would have to go to college. Get a job. Get married. Have kids. Die. Did I want to chuff and chuck, gack and disgorge, spout and spew, barf and blow, huff and heave and hurl my way through life?

No. NO! NOOOOO!

Now was the time to put an end to it all. Now was the time to turn my life around.

If I could refuse to magoo here, now, with a gut full of squirmy, germy vermin and my entire world swallowed up by a stench like no stench the world had ever known, then nothing would ever make me chuck again.

If I could make it here, I could make it anywhere. It was up to me. My dad was right: if I could face this, I could face anything. And it made me feel good to think of my dad in this same position many years earlier.

But the reek wouldn't go away. It assaulted me again, harder than ever. I felt my stomach jerk and jump.

Then it started: hot, buggy vomit surged up my throat!

But I fought back. I forced it back down again.

It counterattacked, stronger than before. I had to heave. I HAD to!

With a supreme effort of will, summoning up all my courage, I held on. I was on my knees, with tears streaming from my eyes, but I did not huff. Me, Robert Warmack, also known as Baby Worm, the world's champion vomiteer, did not let go of a single chunk.

I think I may have passed out for a while because when I awoke, it had grown lighter. Filtered sunlight was glowing dimly through the windows.

I looked around. The room was a mess. But there was no sign of the magoo. I had not heaved. No barfage had taken place.

I stood up. I was feeling a little shaky. The room was still filled with Bigfart's farticane. And even now it was beyond description. But my throat was not doing the wiggle. My stomach was not doing the gack dance.

"I did it," I whispered in amazement. "I DID it!"

I ran over to the door, but not because I was

afraid or sick to my stomach. I just wanted to go out and see the world. The big, beautiful world.

I hesitated, with my hand on the doorknob. This wasn't over . . . yet. There was something I still had to do.

I took a deep, deep breath of Bigfart's stinking air stew. Then I swallowed that breath down into my stomach, where it would mingle with the reek of the bugs and slugs.

Only then did I open the door. Sunlight warmed my face. Birdsong delighted my ears. I felt full of energy, full of vitality. I had vigor. I had tons of vigor.

I walked back across Bigfart's small clearing toward the trees. When I got a few dozen feet away, I paused to look back.

Bigfart's house was gone. There was nothing there but an empty clearing.

I nodded thoughtfully. I didn't know what it all meant, but I nodded thoughtfully just the same. Had it all just been a dream?

I went back to the camp.

It was breakfast time. I could hear the sound of voices coming from the main room.

Breakfast. How that word had terrified me for years. Just the thought of eggs, all runny

105

and yellow and slithery going down the throat, had been enough to send me running for the nearest barf site.

"Ha, Ha!" I laughed out loud. I realized the thought of eggs no longer bothered me. In fact, I would really like to eat some eggs. I could eat a *dozen* eggs.

I stepped up to the doorway. I threw it open like a gunslinger walking into a saloon. And then I swaggered in.

It didn't take long for Hedley to notice me. He was sitting with Buttfire and Jamal. I looked around. Yes, there was Dreezer, just a few seats away.

"Hey, it's Baby Worm," Hedley crowed. "I thought maybe you were still stuck in the outhouse, Baby Worm."

I just stared at him and waited. Slowly the rest of the kids in the room grew silent. They were watching, waiting to see Hedley humiliate me once again. Dreezer was grinning in anticipation.

I spotted Penny. She gave a small wave. I smiled at her.

Once I was sure that everyone was watching, I swaggered over to Hedley. With one hand I pushed Buttfire aside.

"Hey, you better watch it, Baby Worm," Buttfire said.

I sat down directly across from Hedley, ignoring Buttfire's protest.

"Hey, Baby Worm, want some nice, runny eggs?" Hedley asked. He pointed at his plate. There were two sunny-side-up eggs. Two pieces of toast. Hash browns. Sausage.

I'd never had any problem with toast or potatoes, but eggs and sausage had always been in the insta-heave category.

Not any longer.

I reached across the table. I picked up Hedley's fork. I stuck it into one of the eggs and lifted the entire dripping, runny, quivering unborn chicken up . . . up . . . up and popped it into my mouth.

"Everybody run for it! He'll barf for sure!" Hedley cried.

But I reached across the table and grabbed his collar. I yanked him back down into his seat.

"Sit down, Hedley. And shut up."

I believe you could actually have heard a pin drop at that moment. It was dead quiet.

Then Hedley spoke, in his slithery, cruel voice. The voice he used when he was tired of pretending to be halfway human. "You touched me, Baby Worm," he said. "You touched me. And I'm going to kick your—"

"Yeah?" I said. "Then let's do it, Hedley. Come on, let's step outside and settle this like men."

"You don't have the guts," he said. "You'll just heave up your innards before you'll fight me. You're the king of heave, Baby Worm. The biggest coward on earth. A pusillanimous puker."

I nodded. "That's what I *was*, Hedley. But last night, after your little trick with the outhouse, I ran into the woods. And I met someone there."

It was Penny who said it, in an awed whisper: "Bigfart. He met Bigfart!"

"That's right," I said. "I met Bigfart. And I have smelled Bigfart's greatest fart. And I have been changed."

Hedley didn't look so confident anymore. In fact, he looked downright worried. "No way *you* survived Bigfart. No way."

"Way," I said.

"Oh yeah, prove it," he said.

"You know something, Hedley? I was hoping you'd say that." I turned to Penny. "Penny?

You're the only person who has been my friend. You've stood by me. So I have to ask you to step outside."

"But why?" Penny asked.

"Trust me," I said. "Trust me one more time."

She gave me a confident look. "Of course I trust you," she said. She headed for the door.

I guess Dreezer decided that Hedley wasn't handling me well enough, so he sauntered over. He was trying to look especially tough. "Hey, Baby Worm, I told you once before: you mess with the Dreeze, you get the squeeze."

"You can pop that pizza face till you're out of pus, Dreezer," I said. "It won't bother me. I've smelled the smell that destroys the weak. I've smelled the smell of Bigfart's putrid percolating poopfume. I have gone beyond fear and barfing."

"So you say," Hedley sneered.

"You want the proof, Hedley? You can't handle the proof."

"Big talk from a Baby Worm," he said.

"I'll tell you how it happened, Hedley," I said. "There I was, just waking up in Bigfart's cabin. The stench was still all around me. A stench like nothing that has ever been smelled before. Bigfart himself told me it was his greatest and most deadly fart. The reek was trapped in that cabin. And as I was about to leave, I thought to myself: Self, it isn't over yet. It won't be over until everyone who has ever humiliated me and tortured me and called me Baby Worm *knows* that I have changed."

Maybe the crazed look in my eyes made Hedley a little scared. I don't know, but he started to kind of back away.

"Don't move, Hedley," I said. "You asked for proof, you're going to get proof. See, before I left that fetid cabin, I sucked in a bellyful of concentrated reek. It's in my guts now. I *have* Bigfart's fart, and I can release it with a single belch!"

"No!" Hedley cried.

"Ga-hunh?" Jamal said.

"What?" Buttfire asked.

"Yeah, right," Dreezer opined.

"Gentlemen," I said, "prepare yourselves."

I opened my mouth wide. I aimed right for Hedley. And I let go, full force.

BB-UUUU-RRRRR-UUU-HHHUU-URRR-URP!

The fumes of bug and slug stew combined

with distilled essence of Bigfart issued forth from my mouth.

Hedley screamed like a girl and clutched at his throat. "NOOO! NOOOO! NOOOO!"

I loaded up again. BBBUUUGUHUGHUGRRRR-UP!

Dreezer fell to the floor and began writhing like a snake that's been stepped on.

As the fume spread through the room it became a little weaker, but still, the effects were pretty terrible. The heaving and gacking began almost immediately. It was like an orchestra of barf tones and vocals of vomit. It was universal hufferage. Guttal explosions were going off like firecrackers on the Fourth of July.

I turned and walked from the room, carefully stepping over the rising tide of barf that was sweeping across the floor.

Outside, in the clear, fresh air, I found Penny, waiting. She could hear the groans and cries and weeping coming from inside.

"What did you do in there?" she asked.

I laughed. "What did I do? I buried Baby Worm. Come on, Penny. Let's you and me go for a little canoe ride. This time I'll do the paddling."

ELEVEN

So that's the story of how I went from Baby Worm to . . . well, back to being Robert Warmack.

A lot has changed since summer camp. For one thing, I've gained a little weight. It's funny how you can start putting on the pounds once you stop throwing up everything you eat. But mostly it's muscle, because I like to work out a lot now. I have to be in shape for when my dad and I go for hikes in the woods. Next week he's taking me skydiving for the first time. I'm really looking forward to jumping out of a plane.

A lot changed for some other people, too.

Buttfire Tisch found the encounter with my burp to be a life-altering experience. He's not called Buttfire anymore. He's really gotten into the whole school experience. He studies like a fanatic. Study, study, study. Everywhere he goes, he's reading. Of course he still fails every class, but he deserves a lot of support for trying.

Jamal Ishiyama no longer says "ga-hunh." Now he can say "ga" and he can say "hunh," but he has lost the ability to put the two syllables together. I guess that's not a real big change, but there wasn't much for Bigfart's magic to work on in Jamal's case.

As for Dreezer, I never saw him again. No one ever saw him again. I've heard rumors about him. Rumors that he's turned into one of those guys who just sits at home and calls radio talk shows all the time. But that's just a rumor.

And Hedley? Well, Hedley couldn't handle Bigfart's stench like I could. For all his tough talk I guess Hedley wasn't really so tough after all.

The doctors are all baffled. They can't explain what happened. All anyone knows is that Hedley's mind kind of blew out a breaker, if you know what I mean. I guess he couldn't deal with the awful reality. So he retreated in his mind. Back to a time before he encountered Bigfart's deadly stench. In fact, Hedley retreated quite a way. All the way back to babyhood.

They have him in a cradle now. He's wearing diapers. And they say he only ever says two words.

One word is *baby*.

The other word is *worm*.

Glossary of Terms

blew magoo: *noun.* To heave, vomit, extrude, blow, or hurl. As in "I was so sick, I did the blew magoo." The origins of this phrase are lost in the mists of time.

blow: *verb.* To cause stomach contents to surge upward with great force in such a way that they force their way out of the mouth. See also *vomit, hurl, heave,* and *extrude.*

brown substance: *noun.* The basic ingredient that goes into the making of diaper gravy and buttwurst.

brussels sprout: *noun.* Said to have first been developed in Brussels, Belgium, in the sixteenth century. More than four hundred years of effort have failed to wipe it out.

buttal explosion: *noun.* See *farticane.*

butt sausage: *noun.* See *buttwurst.*

buttwurst: *noun.* Named for its resemblance to other members of the "wurst" family, such as brat and knock, the traditional buttwurst differs in that it is not accompanied by either sauerkraut or mustard.

diaper gravy: *noun.* The characteristic product of babies and one of the most deadly substances known to man.

extrude: *verb.* To force out, to push up, to squeeze outward. As in "I extruded my stomach contents."

farticane: *noun.* A fart of great and terrifying power. Farticanes often begin in the Caribbean as a result of the large number plutonium, originally developed as a by-product of the Manhattan Project.

popper: *noun.* A fart that expresses itself in a loud pop. When extended over the course of several seconds, the "popper" becomes a "multipopper."

Pukatao: *noun.* A volcano usually described as being east of Java, it is actually west of Java. Or the reverse.

squeezer: *noun.* A fart that makes an almost plaintive wailing sound.

universal hufferage: *noun.* When a group, party, assemblage, or nation vomits as one.

of elderly cruise ship passengers who consume excessive amounts of shipboard food.

gack dance: *noun*. The characteristic gagging that precedes an episode of hurling.

gumbo: *noun*. Not sure, but believed to involve okra.

guttal explosion: *noun*. An extrusion of stomach contents in an explosive fashion.

heave: *verb*. See *guttal explosion*.

magoo: 1. *noun*. Vomit, stomach contents, lunch revisited, gumbo. 2. *verb*. To huff, hurl, chuck, extrude, vomit, heave, or blow.

ninja fart: *noun*. The ninja fart arrives silently and does its destructive work without warning.

poopfume: *noun*. The aroma of fart.

poop snake: *noun*. See *buttwurst*.

pooptonium: *noun*. A more deadly form of

We hope you enjoyed reading this book. If you would like to receive further information about available titles in the Bantam series, just write to the address below, with your name and address:

KIM PRIOR
Bantam Books
61–63 Uxbridge Road
London W5 5SA

If you live in Australia or New Zealand and would like more information about the series, please write to:

SALLY PORTER
Transworld Publishers (Australia) Pty Ltd
15–25 Helles Avenue
Moorebank
NSW 2170
AUSTRALIA

KIRI MARTIN
Transworld Publishers (NZ) Ltd
3 William Pickering Drive
Albany
Auckland
NEW ZEALAND

All Transworld titles are available by post from:
Bookservice by Post, PO Box 29,
Douglas, Isle of Man IM99 1BQ

Credit Cards accepted.
Please telephone 01624 675137, fax 01624 670923
or Internet http://www.bookpost.co.uk for details

Please allow for post and packing:
UK: £0.75 per book
Overseas: £1.00 per book